DATE DUE

SHAPE YOUR OPINION

Do Kids Have Too Much to Do?

by Jennifer Joline Anderson

Norwood House Press

Norwood House Press
P.O. Box 316598
Chicago, Illinois 60631

For information regarding Norwood House Press, please visit our website at:
www.norwoodhousepress.com or call 866-565-2900.

PHOTO CREDITS: Cover: © mike mols/Shutterstock Images; © 7stock/iStockphoto, 27; © Africa Studio/Shutterstock Images, 8; © Andrey_Popov/Shutterstock Images, 35; © Arina P Habich/Shutterstock Images, 39; © Ermolaev Alexander/Shutterstock Images, 14; © Firma V/Shutterstock Images, 19; © Iakov Filimonov/Shutterstock Images, 32; © Jack Frog/Shutterstock Images, 20; © karelnoppe/Shutterstock Images, 16; © Laszlo66/Shutterstock Images, 25; © mamahoohooba/Shutterstock Images, 10; © matimix/Shutterstock Images, 22; © Patrick Foto/Shutterstock Images, 7; © Rob Marmion/Shutterstock Images, 13; © Sergey Novikov/Shutterstock Images, 40; © SewCream/Shutterstock Images, 29; © Stuart Monk/Shutterstock Images, 4

Hardcover ISBN: 978-1-59953-933-1
Paperback ISBN: 978-1-68404-205-0

Library of Congress Cataloging-in-Publication Data

Names: Anderson, Jennifer Joline, author.
Title: Do kids have too much to do? / by Jennifer Joline Anderson.
Description: Chicago, Illinois : Norwood House Press, [2018] | Series: Shape your opinion | Includes bibliographical references and index.
Identifiers: LCCN 2018003227 (print) | LCCN 2018007258 (ebook) | ISBN 9781684042128 (ebook) | ISBN 9781599539331 (hardcover : alk. paper) | ISBN 9781684042050 (pbk. : alk. paper)
Subjects: LCSH: Play. | Leisure. | Homework. | Children--Time management.
Classification: LCC GV182.9 (ebook) | LCC GV182.9 .A63 2018 (print) | DDC 790.1/922--dc23
LC record available at https://lccn.loc.gov/2018003227

312N—072018
Manufactured in the United States of America in North Mankato, Minnesota.

Table of Contents

Taking music lessons is one way kids spend their time after school.

1

Do Kids Have Too Much to Do?

Kids today have a lot to do! After a busy day at school, many kids take part in other activities. They may go to sports practice. They may have dance class or music lessons. At home, they have homework to do. They may need to do chores, too. In the summer, they might go to day camp. Some people think that with so many activities, kids have too much to do.

Changing Times

In the past, kids spent more time playing with friends. They went outside to play after school. Often, they did not come home until dinner.

But today, more parents have jobs. Many kids stay at after-school programs until parents pick them up. These programs are safe. There is always a teacher or coach watching. But kids have less freedom than they used to have.

"Children are no longer . . . free to roam, play, and explore on their own," explains Peter Gray.[1] Gray is a **psychologist**. He thinks having free time is good for kids.

Against Activities

Many people agree that kids are too busy. They want kids to have more free time. When kids play on their own, they learn to be **independent**. They can make their own fun.

Some experts say kids need more free time to make their own fun.

Being too busy causes **stress**. Kids can feel stressed out by too much homework. They have less time to spend with friends and family. They may not have time to relax and rest.

Trying out different activities gives kids the opportunity to find out what they enjoy doing.

In Favor of Activities

Other people say being busy is good for kids. Kids can learn a lot from sports and other activities. Staying active can help them be healthy. Trying many activities is a good idea.

Kids can find out what they like best. They can also learn new skills. This can make them more **confident**.

EXPLORE THIS BOOK

In this book, three questions about whether kids have too much to do will be examined. *Do kids have too much homework? Are kids too busy with sports? Do kids need more free time?* Each chapter ends with a section called **Let's Look at the Opinions**. This section focuses on points to remember when forming an opinion. At the end of the book, students can test their skills at writing their own opinion essays.

Some schools follow guidelines about how much homework kids of different ages should have.

2

Do Kids Have Too Much Homework?

YES: Kids Have Too Much Homework

Two education groups created the 10-minute rule. They said students should have no more than 10 minutes of homework per night for each grade number. This means fourth graders should have no more than 40 minutes of homework. Fifth graders should have no more than 50 minutes of homework.

In 2015, a report about homework came out. It said kids were getting too much. First graders should have gotten 10 minutes of homework.

Parents said they got 28 minutes. Second graders should have gotten 20 minutes. Parents said they got 29 minutes.

Some elementary schools have chosen to **ban** homework altogether. Students do all their work in school. Then they read a book or spend time with their families each night.

Too Much Homework Can Be Bad

Young kids today get more homework than in the past. One reason is that kids have more tests now. They need to learn everything that will be on the tests. But teachers do not have enough time to teach everything in class. Students have to do work at home to get good grades.

Teachers assign homework so kids can practice and review what they learn at school.

Having more homework doesn't guarantee kids will do better on tests.

However, this may not work. Experts have studied this issue. They found that more homework does not always mean better test scores.

DID YOU KNOW?

Homework amounts differ around the world. In Russia, students average almost ten hours per week. In Finland, they average less than three hours per week. The United States is somewhere in the middle. US students have an average of about six hours of homework per week.

Not only that, but homework can create problems. Students spend a lot of time at school. It may be hard for them to sit still and do homework after they get home. If the homework is confusing, it may cause more stress.

Kids who have too much homework have to give up family time. Without a break from schoolwork, they may begin to not like going to school.

Carol Burris works in education. She thinks homework might not be good for young kids.

Helping with homework lets parents find out what their kids are learning.

She says they should have time to relax instead. Burris says, “I think that giving them a break after 3 o’clock in the afternoon is an awfully good idea.”[2]

No: Kids Do Not Have Too Much Homework

Some parents like their kids to have plenty of homework. Homework helps parents understand what kinds of things their children are learning. That allows them to be more involved with their kids. If their child is having trouble with a subject, parents can help.

Teachers like homework, too. It is a way for kids to review the things they have learned. Kids can show how much they know and understand. Homework sometimes includes work that students do not have enough time to finish at school.

Kids may not want to do homework after a day at school. But doing so is good practice.

They learn study skills they will need when they are older.

The older students get, the more studying they will need to do. Janine Bempechat studies how children learn. She says homework helps kids plan their time and stay focused. She says kids who have homework do better in middle school and high school.

Summing It Up!

Many parents feel kids get more homework than they should. Most young kids don't want to do homework after a full day at school. They want to play and relax. Homework takes away from family time, too. Studies show that homework doesn't always help kids do better on tests. But other parents don't think kids get too much homework.

Giving students homework gives them a chance to practice their study skills.

When kids have too much homework, they have less time with their families.

They think homework helps kids become better students. They think building up study skills sets kids up for success later in life.

Let's Look at the Opinions

FACTS AND OPINIONS

A fact is something a person can prove is true. For example, "First graders have an average of 28 minutes of homework each night" is a fact. This came from a survey asking parents about homework. Facts often include numbers or dates. They can be checked in different ways. These include reading from a trusted source, asking an expert, or doing a survey.

An opinion is a person's own thought, feeling, or belief. Other people may disagree. An opinion might say whether something is bad or good. It might say what people should or shouldn't do. "Kids shouldn't have homework" is an opinion. So is "Homework is good for kids." Opinions need facts to back them up.

Many kids spend a lot of time playing team sports such as soccer.

Are Kids Too Busy with Sports?

YES: Kids Are Too Busy with Sports

Team sports are the most popular out-of-school activities for kids ages 7 to 10. Some of these sports are volleyball, basketball, and soccer. In the United States, 30 million kids from ages 6 to 17 play team sports. Other kids play individual sports, such as tennis or golf.

Many kids play sports all year round. They practice after school. They play on weekends. In the summer, they go to sports camps. Some people say kids can be too involved in sports.

Greg Butler was a professional basketball player. Today, he coaches young kids. "I started playing basketball when I was young," Butler says. "But not as young as kids who are playing sports now. We didn't play ball until fifth or sixth grade. And we certainly didn't play year round like they do today. Kids' sports have gotten out of control."[3]

Sports Put Stress on Kids and Families

Being too involved in sports is not good. It takes away time from other activities. Sometimes kids just want to have fun and not care about winning. Some young athletes play so much they grow tired of a sport. They stop enjoying a sport they once loved.

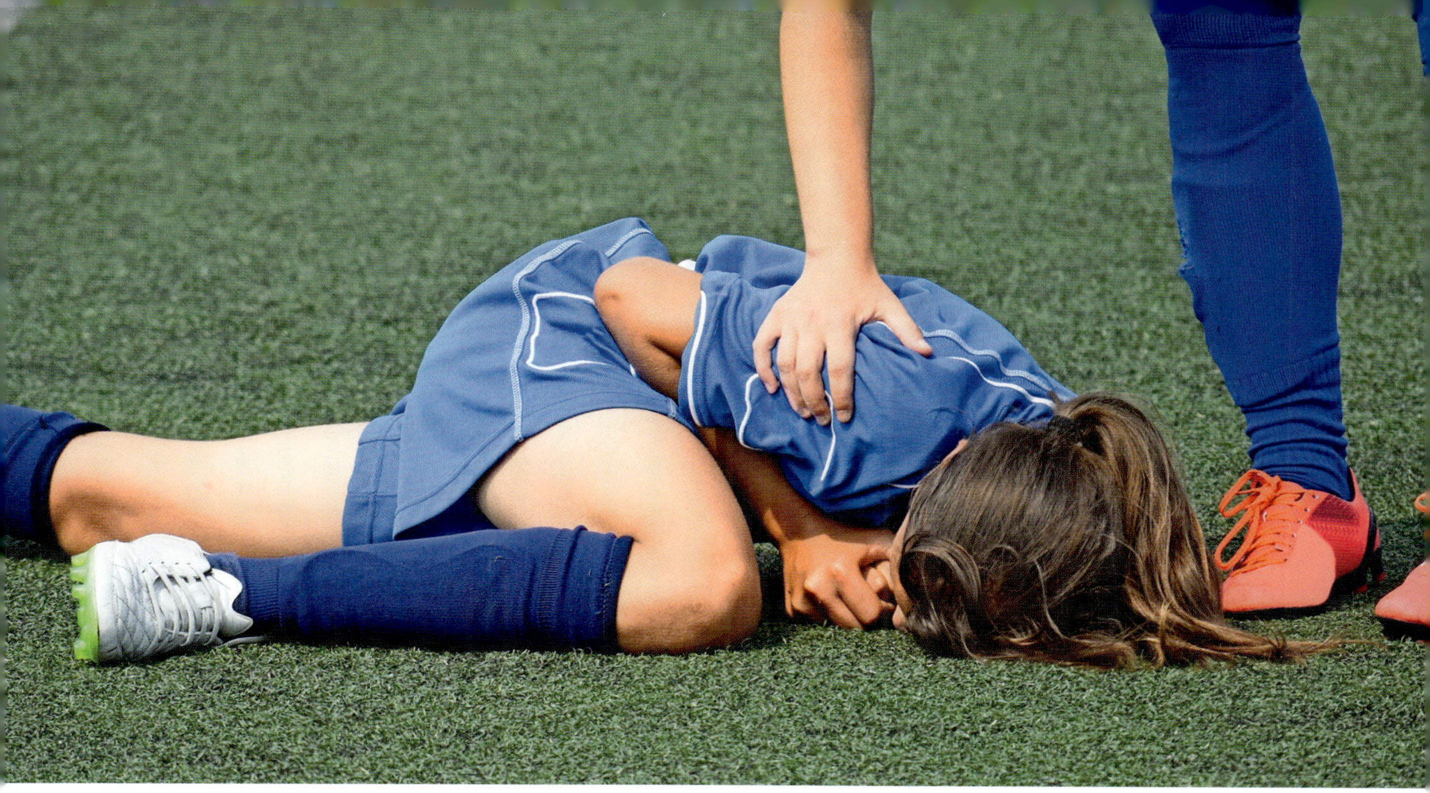

Sports injuries are more likely when kids play a sport for many hours a week.

Too much practice can cause injuries, too. Experts say kids should not practice for more hours than their age each week. For example, a nine-year-old should play no more than nine hours per week. Kids who practice too often are more likely to get hurt. A basketball player might sprain an ankle. A soccer player could bruise a leg.

DID YOU KNOW?

About 40 percent of kids between the ages of 6 and 12 play team sports. The most popular sport is basketball. About 15 percent of kids play it. Next is baseball, with about 13 percent. Third is soccer, with about 9 percent.

NO: Kids Are Not Too Busy with Sports

Should kids be busy with team sports? Most parents say yes! National Public Radio talked to parents in 2015. About 76 percent said they wanted their kids to be in sports. Some even said kids should be more involved, not less.

Sports can help kids stay fit. When kids run, shoot a basketball, or kick a soccer ball, they burn energy. They build stronger muscles. They also improve their skills. They grow more

Sports can help kids become confident in their abilities.

confident about what they can do. Mike Wilber is a youth sports coach. He says, “Young children who are involved in sports have a healthier lifestyle.”[4]

Sports help in other ways, too. Being part of a team teaches kids teamwork. Kids must work together to win. They learn to work hard and do their best.

Amy Roegler is a mom. She has two kids in sports. She says, "When you do sports as a kid, you learn how to win and how to lose. You learn what it's like to put in lots of work and have things not turn out." She also says, "You learn what it feels like to put in a lot of work—and then win."[5] These experiences teach kids how to handle challenges in life.

Summing It Up!

Playing sports is a popular way for kids to spend their time. Some people say kids should not start so early in sports. They also say kids should

Learning what it takes to win is an important lesson kids learn in sports.

not spend so much time on sports. They think families need more time to be together and relax. They worry about kids being hurt when they play sports. Other people think playing sports is a good way for kids to stay healthy. Kids can burn energy and become stronger. Many parents think playing sports helps kids learn how to work with others and do their best.

Let's Look at the Opinions

STRONG ARGUMENTS

An opinion should be supported by a strong argument. A strong argument helps others understand your point of view. It includes reasons that make sense. The first part of the chapter provides a strong argument in favor of playing sports. It says one good reason for kids to join a sport is to keep fit. Another is to learn about teamwork. These reasons make sense.

Sometimes an argument is not strong. It does not include reasons that make sense. For example, "Young kids need to join a sport because everyone else is doing it!" Many parents fall for this idea. They think they must sign their kids up for sports. But the reason does not make sense. Just because many people are doing something does not make it a good idea. When forming an opinion, it is important to use good reasons. A writer should avoid bad ones.

Kids learn how to get along with others when they make up their own games and rules.

Do Kids Need More Free Time?

YES: Kids Need More Free Time

Some people feel kids are not getting enough free time to play. Even recess is shrinking. Many schools have shortened recess. They think kids need more time in classrooms instead. Some have even cut recess completely. This is not good. Kids need recess to burn energy. Recess helps them learn by giving their brains a break.

Playing is more than just a break from school. As psychologist Peter Gray explains, "Playing is learning."[6] Gray says playing helps kids learn independence. They can make their own rules.

DID YOU KNOW?

A survey asked kids to say who chooses their activities. About 62 percent said they picked activities themselves. About 29 percent said they picked activities together with their parents. Only about 9 percent said their parents picked the activities.

They have time to explore their own ideas. When they play with other kids, they become less selfish. They develop **empathy**. They learn to share and get along. Kids find ways to work things out when someone is angry or sad. Not learning these skills makes it difficult for children later in life. This kind of learning happens best when kids play with each other.

Some experts think kids need structured activities to avoid being bored at home.

NO: Kids Don't Need More Free Time

Some experts disagree that kids need more free time. They say kids need more time in school. They believe the school day should be longer.

Some think the school year should be longer, too. They feel more learning will prepare students for future jobs. During the summer, kids forget some of what they learned. Experts worry kids are bored at home and could be using that time for learning.

During the school year, kids may not be as busy as some people say. On average, kids spend only five to seven hours per week in after-school activities. In fact, four out of ten kids do not have any after-school activities at all. These kids may have extra time on their hands and nothing to do.

What are kids doing with all that free time? Some kids do chores at home. Some spend time with family. Others play outside. They may watch

Activities Besides School

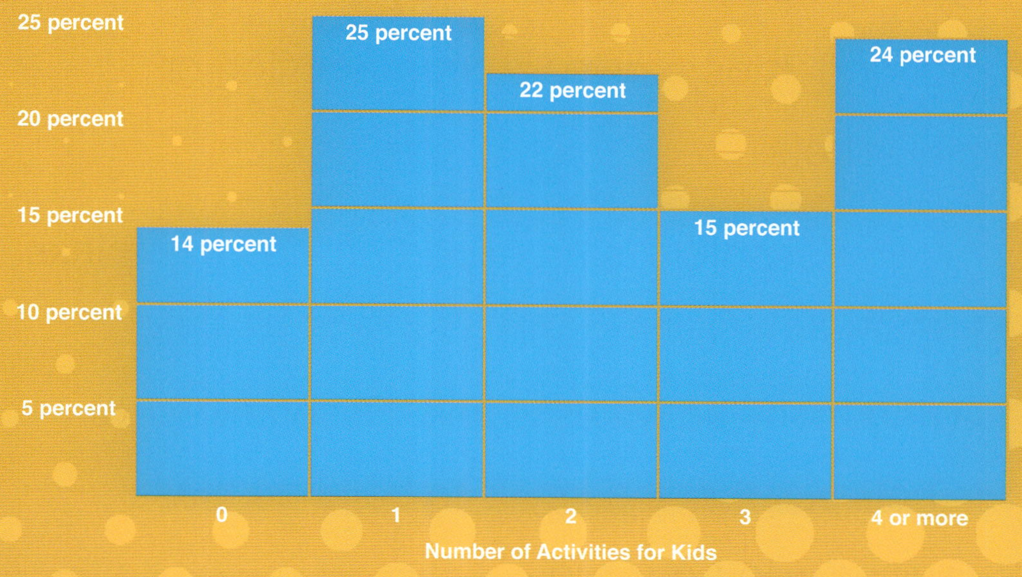

Most kids have more than one activity that they do after school.

TV or play video games. They spend time on their phones. Experts say kids spend more than seven hours a day looking at screens.

Youth activities can get kids away from screens. Kids do fun things in after-school programs. They try new activities and learn new skills. Some kids play sports or take a cooking class. Others may act in a play or learn a new language. Kids can learn programming or build robots.

Alvin Rosenfeld is an expert on kids. He thinks enrichment activities add a lot to kids' lives. Having many activities is fine, Rosenfeld says. He believes that the key is to balance these activities with free time.

Summing It Up!

Some people say kids need more time to play. They say kids learn important lessons by making their own fun. During free time, kids think up their own ideas. They learn how to get along with other

Kids can learn new skills such as cooking in after-school programs.

No matter what they do after school, kids want to have fun!

kids. Other people think kids have enough free time. They think scheduled activities are good for kids. Those activities are fun and teach kids new skills. They help kids put their time to good use.

Let's Look at the Opinions

ASK THE EXPERTS

A good way to support your opinion is to include quotes from experts. These are people who know a lot about a topic. This chapter includes quotes from experts who know a lot about kids' minds. Other chapters included comments from parents and coaches who work with kids.

Expert opinions help support your argument. Opinions by themselves do not prove you are right. However, they make your opinion stronger. They show that others agree with you. When using a quote, be sure to use quotation marks around what was said. Always copy the person's exact words. Be sure to note the website, book, or article where you found the quote.

Write What You Think!

The author shares different opinions in this book. Some opinions state why kids have too much to do. Other opinions argue that kids don't have too much to do. It's important to know many sides of an argument before you form your own opinion.

Opinion writing has a purpose. The writer tries to convince the reader to agree with his or her point of view through different writing methods. One method is to gather facts to support your opinion. Another method is to give reasons that make sense. Yet another is to use quotes from experts. All these methods help make a stronger point.

In writing your own opinion piece, here are six steps to follow:

Step One: *Choose what to write about.*

Pick a subject that interests you. Now think of a question you have about that subject. Decide how you would answer the question. Which side are you on?

Step Two: *Find out more.*

Before you write, find out more about your subject. Read what other people have to say. You could look for research. In this book, experts studied kids' activities and reported the results. Find out the facts. See if an expert has something to say on the subject.

Step Three: *State your opinion.*

The first few sentences should say what your paper is about. You may want to include a question. For example, you could start this way: "This essay is about kids' activities. It asks the question, Do kids have too much to do?"

Next, write down your opinion. You can use phrases such as *I think*, *I believe*, or *in my opinion*. Examples are:

- I think staying busy is good for kids.
- I believe kids should play sports after school.
- In my opinion, kids should have plenty of free time.

Step Four: *Give reasons.*

Opinions should be followed up with reasons for those opinions. When reasons are logical, they influence others to think like you. Come up with two or three reasons why you think the way you do about your subject. Write each reason in a sentence. Use linking words like *because*, *since*, and *therefore* to connect your opinion with the reasons why you came to a certain conclusion. For example, if you are writing a piece on whether kids have too much to do, you might give these reasons:

- I think kids should have more free time, *since* playing with friends helps them learn important skills.
- I think kids should play sports *because* it is healthy for their minds and bodies.

Step Five: *Support your reasons.*

The opinion of a famous person or an authority is a good way to back up your reason. So are results from a survey or research study. Here is an example of how to do this:

First, give an opinion with a reason:

- I think kids should have less homework, since free time will be more useful for them.

Then, give a fact to back up the reason:

- An expert named Carol Burris agrees. She says kids need time to relax after school.

Step Six: *Write the ending.*

Summarize your opinion in the last sentence or two. This makes it clear for the reader what side you are on and why you think the way you do. A good summary wraps up your argument and helps convince the reader to think as you do. You could begin the last sentence with any of these phrases, or you can think of your own:

- For all these reasons, . . .
- As the research indicates, . . .
- To sum up, . . .

GLOSSARY

ban (BAN): To make a rule that something cannot be used or done.

confident (CON-fi-dent): To feel sure about something or about oneself.

empathy (EM-puh-thee): The ability to understand and share another person's feelings.

independent (in-dee-PEN-dent): Acting or thinking on one's own.

psychologist (sy-KOL-uh-jist): An expert who studies the mind and how people behave.

stress (STRESS): A feeling of strain or pressure.

BIBLIOGRAPHY

Books

Gerry, Lisa. *100 Things to Do Before You Grow Up.* Washington, DC: National Geographic Kids, 2014.

Romain, Trevor. *How to Do Homework without Throwing Up.* Minneapolis, MN: Free Spirit Publishing, 2017.

Websites

MedlinePlus: Stress in Childhood

medlineplus.gov/ency/article/002059.htm

PBS Kids: Facts and Opinions

pbskids.org/arthur/games/factsopinions

SOURCE NOTES

1. Peter Gray. "K & Preschool Teachers: Last Stand in War on Childhood?" *Psychology Today.* Sussex Publishers. 8 July 2015. Web. 27 Feb. 2018.

2. Melinda Wenner Moyer. "Are Young Kids Doing Too Much Homework?" *Slate.com.* The Slate Group. 24 Jan. 2017. Web. 27 Feb. 2018.

3. Stephanie Newman. "Kids and Sports: How Much Is Too Much?" *Psychology Today.* Sussex Publishers. 11 May 2010. Web. 27 Feb. 2018.

4. Matt Sloane. "Help Your Child Choose the Right Sport." *WebMD.* WebMD. 2016. Web. 27 Feb. 2018.

5. Patti Neighmond. "Benefits of Sports to a Child's Mind and Heart All Part of the Game." *NPR.* National Public Radio. 1 July 2015. Web. 27 Feb. 2018.

6. Peter Gray. "The Play Deficit." *Aeon.* Aeon Media Group. 18 Sept. 2013. Web. 27 Feb. 2018.

Index

About the Author

Jennifer Joline Anderson is a writer who lives in Minneapolis, Minnesota. She has written many books for young people. She is also a mom of two kids in elementary school.